KT-491-445

Special thanks to Janet Billingham
To Jill and Paulie

ORCHARD BOOKS

First published in Great Britain in 2018 by The Watts Publishing Group

1 3 5 7 9 10 8 6 4 2

Text © 2018 Beast Quest Limited
Cover and inside illustrations by Dynamo
© Beast Quest Limited 2018

Team Hero is a registered trademark in the European Union
Series created by Beast Quest Limited, London

A CIP catalogue record for this book is available from the British Library.

ISBN 978 1 40835 199 4

Printed in Great Britain

MIX
Paper from
responsible sources
FSC® C104740

The paper and board used in this book are made from wood from responsible sources.

Orchard Books
An imprint of Hachette Children's Group
Part of The Watts Publishing Group Limited
Carmelite House, 50 Victoria Embankment, London EC4Y 0DZ

An Hachette UK Company
www.hachette.co.uk
www.hachettechildrens.co.uk

ARMY OF DARKNESS

ADAM BLADE

ORCHARD

MEET *TEAM HERO* ...

JACK

POWER: Super-strength
LIKES: Ventura City FC
DISLIKES: Bullies

RUBY

POWER: Fire vision

LIKES: Comic books

DISLIKES: Small spaces

DANNY

POWER: Super-hearing, able to generate sonic blasts

LIKES: Pizza

DISLIKES: Thunder

CONTENTS

PROLOGUE

URGENT MESSAGE TO ALL HIGHTOWER

LEGION OUTPOSTS,

FROM THE MAYOR OF ASHDALE

CINDERFALL FOREST IS ALIGHT.

SCATTERED SMOKE APPEARED

OVERNIGHT AND NOW A MENACING

PLUME IS GROWING OVER THE FOREST.

WE GLIMPSE SCATTERED FIRES

THROUGH HAZE, COMING CLOSER.

TWO PATROLS SENT TO FOREST TO

INVESTIGATE. NOT RETURNED.

SMOKE SPREADING THIS WAY,

TERRIBLE SOUNDS WITHIN.

FEAR WORSE TO COME. TOWN BEGINNING TO PANIC. ROADS BLOCKED. MUST EVACUATE. PLEASE SEND HELP. PS: PLEASE TAKE CARE OF THE POCKET GRIFFIN CARRYING THIS MESSAGE. HER NAME IS GRISTINA.

CHAPTER 1

WULFSTAN'S CACHE

JACK PEERED through one of the Archive's narrow windows. Outside, the Summer Sea sparkled beneath jagged, snow-capped mountain peaks. Steam wafted up from the clear water.

Jack rubbed his shoulder, as his friend Ruby appeared at his side. "Still sore?" she asked.

Jack grimaced. "Raina almost dislocated it while we were jousting."

Danny looked up from under his fringe of black hair. "You gave as good as you got," he said. "Raina will need time to recover."

"I wonder where she holed up for the night," Jack murmured. He, Ruby and Danny had rested here at Fort Stonetree, after fighting Raina the Vile, an evil shape-shifter. The battle hadn't been easy, but they'd revealed her disguise as Captain Jana, the much-respected Hightower Legion combat instructor at Mount Razor School. And while they hadn't been able to stop Raina from regaining control of her steed, Porphus, the ghost stallion, at least they'd prevented her from causing a volcanic eruption over the town of Bernshoff. They'd defeated her.

For now ...

In the cold light of morning, as Jack stared out at the still-smouldering mountains near Bernshoff, the victory seemed bittersweet. Reunited with her smoke steed, Raina was more powerful than ever.

Ruby picked up Jack's thought. "She could be anywhere."

Jack felt a wave of determination.

"Wherever she is, we'll find her. We've got to stop her before she destroys the Legion and torches the whole world!"

"We've got to rescue Porphus, too," added Danny. "That stallion wouldn't have hurt a fly before Raina turned him into a fire-breathing demon!"

Ruby gestured to the archive's rows of bookshelves. Countless scrolls were squeezed into every available space. "These parchments might hold the key to finding them both."

Suddenly, Ruby gasped. Jack whirled round to follow her gaze.

The face of a snake, almost as big as a man's head, was hovering over

Danny's shoulder. Before Jack could shout a warning to his friend, its forked tongue flicked over Danny's bat-like ear.

Danny recoiled with a screech, startling the serpent. It gave a frightened hiss and lurched backwards. Crest feathers on its head and neck snapped up into its alarm display — a glossy black rosette above two pointed red fans.

Jack bit the inside of his cheek to stop himself laughing. *Poor Danny doesn't think it's funny!*

"Oh, my goodness!" A thin young man dressed in Legion robes hurried towards them, almost dropping the bundle of scrolls cradled in both arms. "Seth! You're meant to be helping me fetch manuscripts, not tormenting Danny!"

"Don't be cross with Seth, Fronn," Jack said to the young sage. "I think he's just worried about Danny. With those ears ..."

Ruby laughed and finished for him. "With his pointed ears, Danny does look a bit like a startled feathered serpent!"

Danny gave a wry grin. "Ha ha, very funny! When the Legionaries told us they were here to protect feathered serpents, I really wanted to see them. I didn't know they'd all want to lick my ears!"

"At least they seem to like you!" chuckled Ruby. "Not like some other beasts I could mention."

"He's a fairly good archive assistant when he's not distracted by ears," Fronn said, turning to the feathered serpent. "Seth, please fetch the scrolls I left by aisle ten."

The serpent smoothed down his feathers and slithered away.

Fronn dropped the manuscripts on the bench. "These are all the histories of Raina I've found so far."

"Shouldn't there be more?" Jack said.

The sage nodded, running his fingers through his thick hair. It stood up on end as if he'd touched an electric eel. "There should be many more manuscripts, spanning centuries."

Jack nodded. "Raina could have destroyed the records while she was in disguise as Captain Jana. No one would have suspected her!"

"Well," Fronn said, "if there's
something to be found, we will find
it here. The archives are as vast and
ancient as the fort itself."

"How old is Fort Stonetree?" Ruby
asked. "It's awesome."

That was true. Jack had never seen
a building like this Legion outpost.
It was built of rough slabs of rock,
like a colossal house of cards, or a
prehistoric stone temple.

The sage puffed himself up. "It is
a thousand years old. Legend has
it that Wulfstan Hightower built it
himself, hefting the slabs of rock with

his bare hands."

Jack nodded politely, thinking, *I've got super-strength like Wulfstan. But I'm not sure I could build something like this.*

His eyes travelled upwards. Apart from the flickering torches and a few faded tapestries, the walls were bare rock. But the slabs of the stone ceiling were painted with a magnificent battle scene.

"Ah, yes," Fronn said, following Jack's gaze. "That's the final battle between Wulfstan and Raina."

Jack studied the mural more closely. In it, Raina had menacing yellow eyes and carried a glowing blue sceptre. She rode a horse that seemed to be made out of dark smoke. Behind her stood ranks of monstrous creatures with bull-like horns.

Fronn went on, pointing to the centre of the painting. "There's Wulfstan, leading his army of Legionaries, and Raina riding her evil steed ..."

"His name's Porphus," interrupted Danny. "And he isn't evil. Not really. We think he's only corrupted when Raina gets her hands on him."

Jack shifted his gaze to the image of Wulfstan. He was wearing magnificent golden armour, and he seemed to loom even larger than the army at his back. "Wulfstan looks so powerful," Jack said. *I'll need to be as strong if I'm going to beat Raina once and for all!*

As if she'd read Jack's mind, Ruby said, "He put Raina out of action for a thousand years."

Jack sighed. "But how?"

Seth reappeared with some manuscripts cradled in a loop of his body. He slithered easily over the floor despite the awkward burden.

Danny began to back away, his eyes fixed on the feathered serpent. "Uh-

uh. My ears are clean enough," he muttered. "I'm out of here." He ran for the door.

Seth's alarm crest sprang up and his black and red feathers quivered anxiously. He dumped the scrolls on the floor and slid out of the room after Danny, crooning a soft hiss.

"That hum Seth's making is one of reassurance," explained Fronn.

"I don't think it's working too well!" Jack laughed.

Suddenly they heard a shout of pain. Ruby's amber eyes widened. "Maybe Seth bites, after all!"

They rushed into the next room,

and Jack breathed a sigh of relief. Seth was trying to smooth Danny's ears down with his forked tongue, but Danny was ignoring him. He sat on the floor, cradling his foot, his back pressed against a large boulder.

"Ran right into that stupid rock," Danny muttered. "Who leaves a boulder in the middle of an archive?"

Fronn looked a little offended. "We believe Wulfstan left it here when he built Fort Stonetree. He even left his mark on it, there ..." He pointed to a large handprint, set in the side of the boulder. "We've tried to move it, but no one's ever been able to."

Jack spread his right palm flat against the cold hard rock. His hand was much smaller than the print, but he felt a tingle of ... *something*. He summoned his strength. The scales of his hand glowed golden. He pushed.

The stone gave a groan and rumbled loudly. Jack felt the slabs tremble under his feet as the monolith slid across the floor, coming to a stop a few paces away.

Fronn spluttered, "How did you … ?"

Jack knelt, running his hands over the stone floor. There was a square shape where the boulder had rested.

"It's a trapdoor!" gasped Ruby. "Can you open it?"

Jack's golden fingers found a metal ring set in a groove. He pulled it. The trapdoor lifted easily, revealing stone steps. Jack peered into the darkness. When he looked up, Fronn was holding a burning torch. His eyes shone with excitement. "I'll go first!" he said, and began the descent.

Jack grinned at Danny and Ruby. "Looks like we're not the only ones who like adventure," he whispered, as they followed Fronn's flickering light.

The steps led into a room made from the same rock as the rest of the fort. It was crowded with objects. Jack could see weapons, armour, tapestries, statues, coins, jewellery ...

"Oh, my goodness," Fronn gasped. "This must be Wulfstan's cache! Legend said he'd hid it in the fort, but I never thought ..."

As they huddled on the only bit of empty floor, Ruby frowned. "It's so cramped in here," she muttered.

Danny grinned. "Looks like Wulfstan was a hoarder!"

Jack ran his gaze over each of the items until he spotted a bowl of gems. They were smooth as glass, and the shade of purple was so dark, they were almost black. Jack picked one up. Something about it was familiar. He was about to ask Fronn about it when

a sudden horn blared, filling the room with noise.

Danny slapped his hands over his sensitive ears. "What's that?" he cried.

Fronn ran for the steps. "It's the call to arms! Something must be wrong!"

Jack dropped the gem into his tunic

pocket, embroidered with the square tower sigil of the Legion.

Jack turned to Ruby and Danny and shouted, "Let's go. It might be Raina!" Then he bounded up the steps after Fronn and Seth as they headed towards the exit, his friends close behind.

An imposing man met them at the door, blocking their exit. A bird-like creature clung to a leather armband on his wrist. It had the head of an eagle, a lion-like body and four taloned legs. It looked like a tiny, winged accifax.

Fronn saluted the man. "Lieutenant Stark!"

Lieutenant Stark nodded coldly

and his eyes flickered over Jack and his friends. "This pocket griffin has brought an urgent message. Cinderfall Forest is on fire. The town of Ashdale needs help evacuating its people. We are the nearest outpost to the town. We must respond immediately!"

"How far is Ashdale?" Jack asked.

"As the griffin flies, very close. It's in the valley below. But as we cannot fly, we take the long road. It is perhaps a four-hour ride, by accifax."

Jack nodded as Ruby and Danny stepped closer. "Then there's no time to lose."

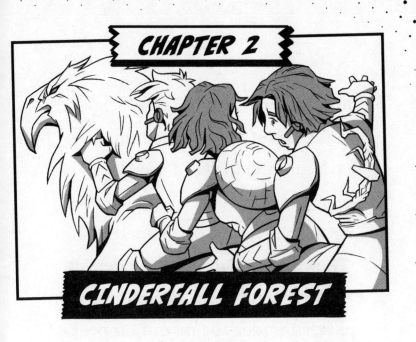

CHAPTER 2

CINDERFALL FOREST

FLINTA THE accifax gave a screech,
and kicked up her hind legs. Jack,
Ruby and Danny all bounced into the
air and dropped back into the saddle.
Danny, in the rear, was thrown higher
than the others, and landed harder.
"Ouch!" he wailed.

Jack scanned the terrain ahead.

Flinta was near the front of the accifax train, close to Lieutenant Stark and the forward scouts. Following them was a long line of Legionaries from Fort Stonetree.

They were heading for Cinderfall Forest. Behind them, the Summer Sea sparkled under the mountain peaks. The Legionaries had explained that a steep wall of cliffs separated the plateau from the valley below. The ridge was impassable, so this track was the only way down.

Jack wondered what they would find in Cinderfall Forest.

Jack spoke into the Oracle hooked

over his ear. "Hawk, sync with Kestrel and Owl so Ruby and Danny can hear too. Tell us about Cinderfall Forest."

There was a brief electronic fizz, and Hawk replied, *"Gladly. Cinderfall is of great historical interest. It is the forest where Wulfstan and his Legion defeated Raina the Vile's army."*

"Eckles told us Raina is part dragon and that she can use fire as a weapon," Ruby said. "Is that true?"

"Yes," said Hawk. *"Though many details about Raina have been lost over the centuries, we know she torched Cinderfall in her battle with Wulfstan."*

"And now the forest is burning

again," added Danny.

Jack nodded. "Raina has to be involved. She's trying to regain her old powers. She's got back one of her eyes and reclaimed Porphus. Now, she's looking for something else."

But what?

At last their path curved to face into the valley. From here, they could see the walled town of Ashdale partly hidden by grey-and-black smoke.

Smoke surged like a river toward the town. Though some of the trees were alive and green, those in the middle were leafless, as if the grey clouds had brought winter with them.

Jack looked at the nearest edge of the forest and shuddered. Something terrible had happened here. While some of the massive trees still stood, their charred trunks cast eerie shadows over the blackened ground. Nothing grew on the forest floor. The trees looked as if they had been like this for aeons. There was something ancient and evil about the ravaged terrain. Ash lay everywhere, thick and still, as if no wind could stir it.

Fronn rode up beside them. "Cinderfall is well named," he said. "All this destruction is from Raina's final battle. The area has remained completely unchanged for a thousand years. Nothing can live in this part of the forest."

"Look!" Jack pointed in the direction of the walled town. A flood of refugees staggered along the road that ran around the edge of the forest. The people were ragged and filthy, with haunted eyes. Many were limping, and some had collapsed at the roadside.

"It's the citizens of Ashdale!" Fronn exclaimed.

"They look like they've been in a war," Ruby whispered.

One man reached up to Lieutenant Stark. "Not everyone got out," he

croaked through dry lips. "Please …
help them!"

Lieutenant Stark nodded curtly then
turned away from the man. He raised
his voice and gestured towards the
forest. "Attention, soldiers! This road is
blocked. We will ride through the forest
to reach Ashdale."

"Wait, Lieutenant!" called Jack.
"Shouldn't we help these people? Or at
least talk to them? They could tell us
what they've seen."

"No time!" Lieutenant Stark growled.
"Our orders are to ensure Ashdale is
fully evacuated, and quickly! The sage
may stay, but we real soldiers have

more important things to do!" He
spurred his accifax into a gallop.

"Whoa," whispered Danny, as the
legion rode directly towards the
blackened trees. "That was kind of

harsh. These people need help!"

"The Legionaries sometimes follow their orders a bit too closely," Ruby muttered. "So what do we do now?"

Jack sighed. "I think we have to follow the lieutenant. Whatever's driving the citizens out of Ashdale must be pretty bad. Odds are that he's going to need our help."

"I will stay here and do what I can for the refugees," said Fronn. "They're going to need medical attention." He gripped each of their hands in turn. When he reached Jack his forehead creased with worry. "Take care in there. I hope to see you all again."

Jack gazed around as they entered the forest. The ruined ground was ploughed up into furrows as if giant wheels had just passed by. Here and there, axe-heads poked up from the earth. The blackened trees towered overhead like broken fangs. The dry smell of ash caught at the back of Jack's throat. Tendrils of smoke writhed between the dead trees, bringing the scent of fresh fire.

It's like the battle was yesterday, not a thousand years ago!

Ruby gasped. "What on ... ?"

Flinta stepped around a great horned skull in their path, and suddenly Jack could see bones everywhere. Huge skeletons were strewn across the ground. Some were half buried. Others were fused to the charred trees as if in the act of uprooting them to use as weapons. With their bull-like horns, they looked like the skeletons of minotaurs. Jack set his jaw. "Raina's ancient army!"

"Correct," said Lieutenant Stark, falling back to ride beside them. "These are all that remain of Raina's terrible horned warriors."

"They've been here for a thousand years?" Ruby asked.

Stark nodded. "The abominable

beasts were left where they fell. The flesh rotted, but not the bones. Even now people avoid the forest. They fear disturbing the bones."

"But we're riding through the forest," Jack said.

The lieutenant scowled at him. "We have no choice. As you saw, the valley road is blocked by the fleeing citizens. I advise you not to get too close to the bones!" He spurred his accifax back to his place at the front of the column.

Jack stared at the horned skeletons and gulped. *They looked formidable. I'm glad they're not alive!*

The smoke thickened as they

passed, and an even denser layer
rolled towards them. It blocked their
path, rearing over them like a wave
edged with ash instead of foam.

One of the accifaxes shied away, and suddenly all the Legionaries were trying to control their jittery mounts.

"I hear something," said Danny. "A kind of screech. It's faint, but horrible. The accifaxes must hear it too."

"I'm glad I haven't got super-hearing like you," Jack said. "The accifaxes are really spooked."

"So am I," Ruby replied. "Can you see shapes in this smoke, or is it just me?"

Jack and Danny squinted into the smoke.

"Definitely shapes," Danny said.

"Not just shapes," said Jack. "Faces! And they don't look friendly."

"You can say that again," Ruby said, lifting her mirror shield as a crazed, snarling face lurched out of the smoke. It reared away and then surged forward again, with more faces looming around it.

Jack drew Blaze from its scabbard. "We're under attack!"

CHAPTER 3

SMOKE ATTACK

FLINTA SNAPPED her beak
nervously at the twisting smoke. Jack
could hear a noise like fingernails on
rock. He gripped Blaze tightly and
glanced back at the others. Ruby's
eyes glowed amber, and Danny had
an energy bolt fitted in his crossbow.
They both looked frightened.

"Smoke can't hurt us," said Jack, but he wasn't sure.

One of the Legionaries screamed. He swung his sword wildly, staring back over his shoulder as his accifax began to run. The smoke parted in front of him and Jack saw the shape of a huge tree loom out of the shadows.

"Stop!" Jack yelled.

But it was too late. *Whump!* The accifax ran straight into the giant, fire-hardened tree. Jack flinched as the rider and his mount crumpled to the ground.

Jack scanned the crowd of bucking accifaxes, looking for the lieutenant.

There!

Lieutenant Stark was in the middle of the chaos yelling, "Halt! Hold fast!" But no one was listening, not even the lieutenant's accifax. It tripped and fell, disappearing in a plume of ash and smoke into a hidden pit.

Other Legionaries tumbled to the ground, sending up puffs of ash as they sprawled flat, or vanishing completely into the pits.

"I'll get everyone's attention," said Ruby, flashing her eyes upwards and sending two beams of orange light towards the sky. A few of the soldiers looked up.

"The smoke is filled with illusions!"
Jack yelled to the others. "The faces

aren't really there!"

But the Legionaries'
accifaxes were
already panicking,
and the soldiers
staggered between
the animals' sharp,
raking claws and the
spectral shapes in the
smoke. Only Flinta
stayed quiet, pawing
the ground but holding steady.

Jack watched helplessly as the
rest of the Legionaries scattered.

The smoke parted for the accifaxes as they bolted towards the valley road, back the way they'd come. The riders who had been thrown by their bucking mounts sat on the ground, wailing and throwing punches at twisting smoke.

Jack shook his head. "The smoke is driving everyone crazy! It's trying to stop us going deeper into the forest."

Ruby's amber eyes flashed. "You're right. But why?"

"It must be Raina," said Jack. "I bet there's something in there that she doesn't want us to know about. We have to find out what it is."

Suddenly, Ruby gave a strangled shout of fear.

Jack spun around and was horrified to see Ruby's head hidden by smoke. Jack could hear her rasping breath as she struggled to breathe through the suffocating mask. Danny raced towards her, but a rope of smoke tangled around his ankles and he fell to the ground.

Blaze felt impossibly heavy. With an effort, Jack gathered his superpower. His hands glowed golden as strength flowed into them. He lifted the sunsteel blade to the smoke around Ruby's head. At the touch of the magical blade, the smoke peeled away. Ruby gasped and rubbed her neck. "Thanks!" she rasped. "Looks like the smoke's not just illusions after all!"

Jack cut through the rope-like vapours binding Danny's legs. Then he whirled around, stabbing and slicing at the surrounding smoke. The smoke withdrew from wherever the sword touched it, but for only a few moments.

It keeps coming back!

Just then a gap appeared in the writhing smoke. At the same time, there was a break in the clouds overhead. Sunbeams poured through the tree branches and bounced off Blaze in a flash of light. A patch of smoke recoiled from the glare.

"Look," said Ruby, pointing out the retreating smoke. "It doesn't seem to like the light."

But the gap in the clouds closed as quickly as it had opened, plunging them back into a grey haze. "There goes the sun," sighed Jack.

"We may not have sun, but we do have sunsteel," Ruby said, her amber eyes shining. "And you've got me! Jack, hold up Blaze!"

Jack looked at her, catching on to her plan. *Of course!*

He held Blaze at arm's length. Ruby's eyes glowed with fire, and she shot twin beams of orange flame at the sword. Jack held the sword steady as the light bounced off the sunsteel blade. Wherever the reflected beams touched smoke, it withdrew.

Without breaking the fiery beams flashing from her eyes, Ruby angled her mirror shield. It reflected some of the light from Jack's sword, fanning it out into a broader beam, repelling even more smoke.

Jack and Ruby quickly cleared a wide area around them. Gradually the smoke receded and the panicked

Legionaries began to calm down.

"Somebody get me out of here!"

Lieutenant Stark shouted grumpily

from the pit where he was trapped.

"We'd better help him," Jack said. He and the others hurriedly pulled the lieutenant and the rest of the Legionaries to safety.

When the last of the soldiers were gathered up, Jack pointed Lieutenant Stark back towards the road. "The smoke won't stay away for long," he said. "Head back to the road. Look out for any refugees that may have come this way. We'll meet you at Ashdale."

Stark nodded. "What about you?"

Jack glanced at Ruby and Danny. They were already mounted on Flinta, waiting for him.

"Flinta held while the rest of the

accifaxes bolted," Jack said. "She'll take us on through the forest. The sooner we get to Ashdale, the sooner we can help those who are left."

Jack was right. Flinta trotted boldly through the forest as her riders kept the smoke at bay. They soon left the charred battleground behind and came to living trees.

But still the forest was eerily silent. The evil smoke hovered out of range of their magical weapons. Ghostly faces hovered within it, but cringed back into the gloom as Jack and his friends passed by.

At last, they rode out from the

trees and saw Ashdale ahead. Part of the strong, defensive outer wall that circled the town was wrecked.

"It's been blasted," said Danny.

"Well, at least we don't have to find the town gates," Ruby said. "We can ride right through the wall!"

Flinta clambered over the rubble and carried them into the town. Like the wall, the nearby buildings had collapsed. The streets were full of abandoned belongings.

"It's deserted," Ruby said.

"Not quite," Danny replied. "I can hear people shouting for help!"

Flinta galloped through the streets,

following Danny's directions. Soon they could all hear the shouts, and when Flinta skidded round a corner, Jack saw the last survivors of Ashdale, cowering with their backs to the walls. Advancing on them were powerful, lumbering creatures, waving giant axes over their bull-like heads. Their horns glistened and their burnished muscles shone red.

Danny gasped in horror. "Raina's horned warriors!"

"It can't be! They've been dead for centuries," Ruby said.

As if to prove her wrong, one of the minotaur-like creatures turned, very much alive. Jack felt a wave of heat. His heart turned over. The beast opened its mouth to show a throat full of fire. Flame shone from holes where its eyes should have been. Its horns were edged with fire! And what Jack had thought were muscles were red-hot cinders smouldering between its ribs and along its limbs. This was not a flesh and blood creature ...

It was made of embers and bone.

CHAPTER 4

EMBER WARRIORS

ONE BY one, the ember warriors
turned to face Jack and his friends.
Fire sparked off ridges on their horns.

Jack slid off Flinta's back and
nudged her away. He stood beside
Ruby and Danny as the warriors
began to move. The road shook with
each step of their great hoofed feet.

Danny eyed them. "That's a lot of hot air heading for us!"

"Let's blow it away!" Jack said, reaching for his blade.

Danny let loose an energy bolt from his crossbow. It found a target where the creature's heart should be. The red embers between its bones flared and then the beast disintegrated into a pile of ash.

Two warriors came at Jack. The first lifted its axe and smashed it down at Jack's head. Jack darted aside, and the blade whistled past his ear. He twisted and lunged with Blaze, stabbing the warrior through

its smouldering ribs. His sword
was still buried in the creature's
chest as Jack whirled round to face
the second warrior.

POW! He thumped a golden fist
into its stomach. The super-strength
punch sent the monster flying
towards a house, its bones flaring
with fire.

Crash! It smashed through the wall,
and the flames went out as the roof
collapsed on top of it.

"Nice one, Jack!" Ruby panted,
spinning her shield. The knife-like
spikes set around the edge sliced into
the warrior she fought.

"You too, Ruby!" said Jack, as he dodged another swinging axe head. "These things mean business!"

Ruby grunted, "So do we!" as she ducked under the flailing arm of another beast. Just in time, she blocked a blow it had aimed at Danny, who was busy firing energy bolts as more monsters emerged from the surrounding buildings. Jack almost smiled. In a fight for his life, there was no one he'd rather have beside him than Ruby and Danny.

The street was littered with piles of ash and horns. The remaining warriors began to spread out.

"They're trying to surround us," Jack said. "We need to cut them off."

"I've got this side," said Ruby, firing her flame-beam eyes to the right. "But they just keep coming!"

"I'm going to use my sonic blast," Danny said. Jack covered his ears as Danny opened his mouth and screeched. A wave of supersonic energy slammed into the warriors. The nearest ones began to shake, belching fire as their bones vibrated, before they burst apart and scattered in a rain of fiery ash.

Jack squinted through the cloud of ash and sparks. Three warriors were left, and they were almost twice as tall as their fallen comrades. Jack had to crane his neck to take in the sheer size of them. He whistled through his teeth.

One of the giant warriors reached over its shoulder and pulled out a great iron club. Jack gulped. It was almost as tall as he was!

SCHLOOP! The club circled towards Jack's head. Without thinking, he raised his free hand. He felt the jolt all the way down to his toes as his super-strength blocked the blow. Then he shoved. The club swung back, taking the warrior by surprise. It slammed into its arm, twisting it around. Danny followed up with a bolt from his crossbow. The warrior flared and died.

The two remaining giants hesitated, looking wary of the magical weapons facing them.

"Try your sonic blast again, Danny,"
Jack whispered.

Danny screeched. The warriors
stumbled backwards, but they were
stronger than the smaller beasts and
did not disintegrate. Jack, Danny and
Ruby herded them along the narrow
streets until they were backed up
against the town wall. They were
almost as tall as the wall!

"Lucky it's not the demolished bit!"
said Danny. Jack agreed. The wall
here was strong. And it had steps
leading up to the battlement. Jack
took the steps two at a time, while
Danny and Ruby kept the beasts

busy below. Jack slashed Blaze
through the base of a warrior's horns.
The creature disintegrated in a rain of
sparks and ash.

Jack turned to the next one.
"Keep it busy!" he yelled to Danny
and Ruby. The warrior swung its
club. While Danny and Ruby dodged
aside, Jack pounced to stab Blaze
down into the point where the
embers of its shoulder met its neck.
The horrible creature screamed,
and flames swept from its fiery
throat out into the street. Jack
pulled back for a second blow, but
the warrior was finished.

Ruby high-fived Danny, and Jack pumped the air with a golden fist. "We did it!"

Suddenly Raina's voice rang out. "I trained you well, Jack!"

Jack whirled round. All he could see from the battlements was the veil of smoke smothering Cinderfall Forest. There was no sign of Raina the Vile. Yet her voice thundered from somewhere inside the black cloud. "But all your training will be useless against my full force. My loyal warriors are rising to my cause, after sleeping for a thousand years. You have met only a few of them. Soon I will once more have full control over them all." Raina gave a crazed laugh. "And then I will be unstoppable! The Legion will be helpless. And you will be helpless too, Chosen One!"

Raina fell silent. Jack turned his back on the forest and looked down at his friends' anxious faces.

"So," said Danny, "we have to face more of Raina's warriors."

"Maybe," said Jack. "But from what she said, she hasn't got full control of them. So we've got time to stop her before things get any worse!"

He spoke into the Oracle hooked over his ear. "Hawk, I can't see through the smoke. Can you scan the valley for thermal signals, please?"

"Yes, Jack," replied Hawk. A visor slid out over Jack's eyes, and Hawk projected the thermal profile of the

landscape on to the viewscreen.

Jack studied it. "There are heat spots everywhere," he muttered.

"Indeed," agreed Hawk. *"But there is a major concentration in one particular location."* The screen zoomed in on an area that seemed to be bursting with red.

Jack nodded. "Whatever Raina's up to is happening there." He hurtled down the steps to Ruby and Danny. "I know where we have to go. Let's get Flinta!"

They found their loyal accifax waiting for them, and they rode through the ruins of the empty streets to the town gates. The great wooden doors were scattered in pieces over the ground.

As they scrambled over the wreckage, a squad of Legionaries stumbled through the gateway. Most were on foot and looked haggard and exhausted. Jack recognised Lieutenant Stark riding at the front, and the other leader too: a tall, blonde woman in armour who sat ramrod-straight on her accifax.

"It's Commandant Eckles," Jack said. "Her squad must have met up with Lieutenant Stark's on the road!"

"Good," said Ruby. "We finally have some real help!"

But neither of the Legion's officers looked pleased to see Jack and his friends. Both leaders regarded them with stony expressions.

"Raina is raising an army," Jack told them. "The horned warriors are different — worse than before. She's not fully in control of them yet, but—"

Commandant Eckles glared at Jack. "Young man, whatever Raina is or isn't in control of, it's clear that Cinderfall Valley has fallen to the enemy. This battle is lost."

"But … there's still hope, Commandant," Jack stammered. "If we can just—"

Commandant Eckles forged on. "My division barely managed to fight our way here, even with Lieutenant Stark's forces. My strategy now is to make sure every last person has been evacuated from Ashdale, and then withdraw from the valley."

She raised her voice so the Legion could hear. "We will return. Once we have regrouped, we will face Raina army to army."

The Legionaries straightened their shoulders and mustered a cheer. Commandant Eckles smiled around at them. "A battle for the ages!" she cried. "We will fight Raina and her horde just as Wulfstan himself did!" There were a few more cheers.

Jack shook his head. Didn't they understand? If they waited to regroup, Raina would be too powerful to defeat.

"Please listen," Jack pleaded. "We can stop this war before it starts. My Oracle detected a concentration of heat in the forest. I think—"

Commandant Eckles snorted. "I am not interested in what you — or your little gadget — think. When this is over we will have a long talk about your recent conduct."

Jack was confused. "My conduct?"

"I told you it was forbidden to touch the Orb of Foresight, yet you did.

You then failed to alert the Legion
to Raina's plan to enter the caverns
of steam. Had you followed protocol,
we could have helped you stop her."
Commandant Eckles' eyes were cold
and furious. "You think you're a hero,
when you're actually just a vain,
boastful boy."

"Hey!" interrupted Danny. "Jack isn't
vain or boastful. And he *is* a hero!
We didn't tell the Legion about Raina
because we were afraid she was in
disguise at Mount Razor ..."

"Which she was!" added Ruby.
"She's been hiding under your nose as
Captain Jana for years!"

Commandant Eckles scowled down her nose at the three friends.

"It is not your place to criticise the Legion!" she barked. "You are here to obey orders and help with the evacuation. I will deal with you later!"

She turned and rode away.

"Well, that went well," said Danny dryly. "And meanwhile Raina is out there forming her army."

"It's not too late to stop her. Not yet," said Jack. He grinned at his friends. "We're going to get to the source of the heat in that forest, even if it means disobeying orders!"

CHAPTER 5

THE INFERNO SCEPTRE

LEGIONARIES PATROLLED
Ashdale's entrance, but Jack had
been watching them carefully. He
knew when to ride Flinta out without
being detected. Even with Jack, Ruby
and Danny on her back, the accifax
was fast and quiet.

The thickening cloud of smoke

hovered over their heads as they crossed the valley and went on into the forest. When Jack glanced back, he saw the haze rolling slowly after them. He shuddered.

"Creepy!" Ruby's voice was hoarse.

They heard a sudden, deep grating noise from somewhere in the distance. Danny lifted his crossbow.

The smoke gathered as they rode deeper into the forest. Suddenly a black tide of smoke flowed over their heads, almost close enough to touch.

Jack jabbed his sword skywards at the same time as Danny fired an energy bolt. The smoky soot disintegrated into writhing tendrils.

"Good shot!" Ruby said. She blasted another black wave with her flame-vision. Soon they were all busy keeping the fearsome smoke at bay.

The cloud was a black fog by the time they entered the ancient battleground. It hung like ghostly grey foliage over the charred trees.

"Hawk," Jack said. "Sync with Kestrel and Owl. Give us thermal vision."

"Of course, Jack," Hawk replied. *"I was wondering when you would ask."*

Their visors slid over their eyes. Ruby's had slits in it to allow her to fire her flame-vision.

Jack scanned the heat pattern
displayed in front of
him and pointed. "The
centre of the heat is
over there!"

The forest seemed
to groan as they
urged Flinta forward.
Jack saw a shape
forming within the
heat-spot on his visor.

"Slow down, Flinta," he whispered.
"We don't know what we're going to
find. It looks like a huge tree. But
there's more ..."

"It's surrounded by other shapes,"

Danny said. "Are they smaller trees?"

"I don't think so ..." Jack urged
Flinta a little closer through the dead
trees. It was hot in the forest, but a
cold shiver ran down his spine as he
recognised the figures.

"It's Raina and Porphus, and a bunch
of ember warriors," he murmured.
"Hawk, withdraw the thermal vision."
The visors slid back. The fires
smouldering inside Raina's fiery steed
and the ember warriors were clearly
visible to their unaided eyes.

The warriors were clustered round
the giant tree. Its bark was charred,
and the whole tree glowed red-hot with

inner fire. Its branches were crooked as if they had been twisted into place, and they were tipped with flames instead of leaves. Flares of light burst from its trunk like jets of blood as the warriors hacked at it with their axes.

"They're chopping it down!" whispered Ruby.

Raina's voice rang through the forest. "Faster!" she commanded. "Wulfstan buried my Inferno Sceptre here. I know it! Only the Sceptre could give a tree the energy to grow so immense! It's almost within my grasp!"

The Inferno Sceptre! Jack cautiously urged Flinta on. The sparse trees

gave little shelter. He remembered the red staff the villain wielded from the mural he'd seen in the archive at Fort Stonetree. *She mustn't find it!*

"Look out!" Danny yelled. Flinta shied as ember warriors lurched out of the smoke on both sides.

"Down!" Jack shouted, flinging himself after Ruby and Danny as an axe hissed over his head. Jack hit the ground and twisted, striking a warrior with Blaze. The sunsteel sword slashed through its leg bones and it disintegrated in a burst of fire.

Jack lifted Blaze and struck again, slicing another axe out of a skeletal hand. Beside him, Ruby and Danny fired their weapons into more of the warriors. Raina spun her steed round to face the fight. She wore a dark cloak and an Orb of Foresight glowed yellow in one of her eye sockets.

"Ha!" Raina shouted. "No doubt you wish to view the Sceptre before you die. Let us see if you can last that long!"

Some of the ember warriors carried on chopping at the great, glowing tree, while others joined the attack.

Danny was reloading his crossbow when a warrior brought its axe down towards his shoulder. Jack swung Blaze up. The sunsteel blade sliced through the attacker's wrist. Flames shot from the warrior's severed arm. Jack thrust his sword into its body, and a wave of heat stung his face as the creature collapsed into ash.

"Thanks!" Danny said, and carried on firing.

Porphus raised the hooked horns that had once been his ears. He snorted, and a stream of blue flame shot from his mouth. His blazing hooves kicked at the blackened ground, scorching it more. Raina drew her sword as the smoky steed leapt forwards.

"You two keep the warriors busy!" yelled Jack. "I'll take Raina!"

Raina threw back her head and roared with laughter. "Well, then, young 'hero'. Let's make it a fair fight!" She leapt off Porphus's back and stood facing Jack, her sword held high.

Jack swallowed. Raina wielded powerful magic. As Jana, the martial arts instructor of Mount Razor, she was also a master at combat. She charged, and he was only just able to parry her strike in time. The collision sent a tremor through his whole body.

Taking a deep breath, Jack gathered his super-strength and his hands grew brighter. He blocked one after another of Raina's fierce blows. The jarring shock of each impact was less now, but still Raina was slowly pushing him backwards. Jack fought on, blindly stumbling backwards with every stab of Raina's sword.

Raina began to charge at him, but then skidded to a stop, staring past Jack. He spun round to follow her gaze. Their fight had brought him closer to the great tree. Danny was a little in front of him, and Ruby off to his left. The battle had stopped. The attacking warriors stood frozen, gazing at Raina. The creatures that had been chopping the tree stepped back. Then Jack heard a dreadful groan, and the massive trunk tilted ... towards Danny!

Jack hurled himself at his friend. They landed, and Jack felt a gust of wind like a punch as the giant tree crashed to the ground beside them.

Jack sat up and looked past the fallen tree. The severed stump in the ground had split to the roots. The force had cracked open the scorched earth around it. A fiery red sphere lay half-buried under the surface. Jack recognized the object from the mural on the archive ceiling at Fort Stonetree.

The Inferno Sceptre!

With a cry of triumph, Raina leapt forward and seized the flaming sceptre. Red streaks of energy pulsed out of it and twined around her wrist. Raina held it up, cackling in delight.

The broken trees around her burst into flames.

All around them, the charred, ashy landscape was splitting open. Horned warriors began to climb up out of

the earth, and Jack's stomach gave a sickening lurch.

More and more of them came. At first they were cold bones, but then their fire ignited. Soon there were hundreds of glowing ember warriors advancing through the trees of the ancient burned forest.

Danny gulped. "It's an entire army!"

"Against three of us!" said Ruby.

Jack readied Blaze. Their odds weren't good, but if they were going down, it wouldn't be without a fight.

CHAPTER 6

FLOOD

"THIS," RAINA said, "is how it will be when I am ruler. The world on fire!"

Next to Jack, a warrior swung its axe at Ruby. She blasted it with her flame vision, while Danny fired a constant stream of energy bolts. But for every warrior they destroyed, there were twenty more to take its place.

"Look out, guys," warned Danny. "I'm going to make some noise."

Jack and Ruby covered their ears as Danny loosed his sonic blast. The sound burst out, reducing the nearest warriors to clouds of sparks and ash.

More warriors immediately started forward. Danny reloaded his crossbow. "We need a fire hose," he muttered.

A fire hose ...

Jack immediately had an idea. "You're a genius! Get out of the valley, as high as you can! I have a plan."

The accifax appeared at his side like magic. Jack grinned and leapt on to her back. "Great hearing, Flinta!" He galloped away from the battle, out of the forest, straight for the steep cliffs that reared up under the plateau of the Summer Sea.

The cliffs were stark white, but the glare from the forest fire seemed to stain them with blood. They were much too high and steep to climb.

Jack dismounted at the foot of the cliffs. He patted Flinta. "Thanks," he said. "Now, find Danny and Ruby. Help get them up to high ground."

Flinta let out a trill, puffed out the feathers of her head, then whirled round and bounded from sight.

I hope she understood me!

Jack turned back to the cliffs, his hands beginning to tingle as he summoned his strength. The scales shone brilliant gold. *THUMP!*

With one powerful strike, he punched a hole in the cliff wall. Rocks tumbled to his feet, and he scrambled up on to them to punch the cliff again, working like a bulldozer, tearing into the rock. And with every punch he climbed higher and deeper into the cliff.

He couldn't tell how much time passed before he broke through the ground level of the plateau above. Exhausted, he peered back down. He had created a channel that ran from the base of the cliffs right to the top. Raising his eyes, he could make out the edge of the Summer Sea sparkling, just a few metres away across the plateau.

Gathering the last of his strength into his golden hands, Jack tore through the last of the rocks, throwing himself aside with the final slab of stone at the last moment.

The water of the Summer Sea rushed past him into the channel, cascading down the cliff.

Exhausted, Jack watched the massive waterfall rush into the forest below. The unleashed waters of the Summer Sea surged through the

burning forest, with a strength that
was as relentless as the tide. Clusters
of huge, burning trees were snuffed
out in a moment. Jack saw a squadron
of ember warriors overcome by the
crest of the water and vanishing into

tiny whisps of steam as they were extinguished. In less than a minute, what had been a burning valley became a soggy landscape filled with nothing more sinister than a haze of smoke.

"Jack!"

Jack lifted his head. It was Danny and Ruby riding Flinta up the cliff-top towards him. The accifax nuzzled his cheek as Danny and Ruby dismounted. Danny hauled Jack to his feet.

"Whoa, Jack! You just flooded an entire valley — and defeated a whole army — single-handed!"

Jack smiled in relief and gave them both the gentlest of arm-punches.

His golden hands were fading fast. "*We* defeated a whole army! You two were brilliant."

But then Ruby recoiled, staring at him in horror, "Ugh! What on ... ?"

Danny stepped back too, his frowning face full of confusion. He pointed wordlessly at Jack's pocket. Jack stared down. Black shadow was billowing out of his pocket.

Noxxian shadow!

Jack drew his sword. "Stay back!"

The shadow twisted into an arrow-shaped cloud. It headed towards Danny and Ruby, as if it knew they were more vulnerable than Jack.

"Oh, no, you don't," Jack growled. He drew his sword and the sunsteel blade sliced through the evil cloud with a sizzle The cloud twisted, writhing around Jack's arm and neck, but it couldn't hurt him. It melted into wisps with every stroke of his sword, and the wisps vanished like dirty steam.

At last the air was clear.

Ruby nodded. "It's lucky you're immune to shadow, Jack. It almost got Danny and me!"

"But how was it in your pocket?" asked Danny.

Jack reached into his pocket, feeling a few sharp fragments of ...

The dark gem from the Archive!

He showed his friends the broken pieces. "It was the gem I found in Wulfstan's cache under the Stonetree archives. It must have got smashed in the battle."

"But why did shadow come out of it?" Danny said.

Jack shuddered. "The only explanation is that the gem was Noxxian. But if Wulfstan was using Noxxian shadow, then—"

A terrible thought began to take shape in Jack's mind.

No, it can't be!

"What is it, Jack?" Danny asked.

"I wasn't sure what it meant at the time, but in my vision with the Orb of Foresight, there was a moment when I saw Wulfstan's eyes," Jack said. "And I could have sworn that I saw a flash of red in them."

"Red eyes?" Ruby asked. "You mean, just like ..." Her jaw went slack with horror at what Jack meant.

"Hawk," Jack said, speaking to his Oracle. "Show me some images comparing Wulfstan and General Gore."

"Certainly," Hawk replied, as the visor slid across Jack's eyes. *"But I must caution you against jumping to conclusions. There are no accurate*

measurements for Wulfstan's height and weight."

"Understood," said Jack, scanning the pictures. "But that's not what I'm looking for. That is!"

"What?" Ruby asked.

"Hawk — send these images to Owl and Kestrel. Look at Gore's helmet. There's a jewel mounted on it, and it's dark purple, almost black." Jack looked over at his friends. "It's identical to the gems we found in Fort Stonetree."

"And we found them in Wulfstan's cache," Danny said, nodding slowly, eyes widening as the full meaning of this dawned on him.

"Exactly!" Jack said. " If Wulfstan had jewels infused with Noxxian shadow, then he was using magic from the underrealms! The Hero Wulfstan Hightower became the villain General Gore! They're the same person!"

But before Jack could fully absorb this shock, Commandant Eckles and Lieutenant Stark galloped up to them. The two were riding

at the head of their combined forces, escorting the last of the refugees towards Fort Stonetree. Jack could see Matthias, the head boy of Mount Razor School, riding near the front. Fronn was at the back, among the refugees.

The Commandant pulled her mount up short and fixed Jack with a glare. "You disobeyed my direct order!"

But before Jack could respond, a cry of fear rose up from the Legionaries and refugees.

Jack spun round. A final tendril of smoke was rising from the centre of the valley, forming a face in the sky.

Raina!

The dreadful mouth twisted, and Raina's voice bellowed out. "Yes, Commandant. You are right to reprimand our young 'hero'. He is becoming arrogant as his power grows."

Commandant Eckles looked as if she had swallowed a lemon.

Raina continued, "And do you know what happens when heroes get too powerful? They become corrupted. Just look at what happened to Wulfstan Hightower."

"What of our founder, Lord Hightower?" croaked Commandant Eckles, looking paler by the second.

Raina gave an evil cackle. "One

thousand years ago, Hightower's power
consumed him. Your precious founder
became the world's greatest villain!
Wulfstan Hightower became tired
of being a hero. And that's when he
became General Gore!"

The Legionaries began to shout in disbelief and anger.

Raina's smoke cloud was fading fast, but her voice still rang out. "Your worthless Legion is built on a lie. Once I have regained the last of my powers, I will burn it to the ground!" The remaining smoke blew away and Raina was gone.

Commandant Eckles looked stunned. "R-r-rubbish," she stammered. "I don't believe a word of it." She turned to rejoin her men. "Courage, Legion. Our enemy spreads lies to confuse us!"

Jack raced after Commandant Eckles, his friends just a few paces behind.

"Wait!" called Jack. "Raina was telling the truth about Wulf—"

The Commandant cut him off. "Be quiet! Spreading lies about our great founder is unforgiveable at any time. During such a crisis as this, it is the last straw. My experiment with using 'heroes' to do the Legion's job is clearly a failure. You are all expelled!"

Wait ... what?

Jack was too stunned to speak as Commandant Eckles rode away. He shook his head, trying to gather his thoughts.

Danny lightly cuffed his arm. "Don't let her get to you, Jack."

Ruby added, "She's the loser here, not us."

Jack looked at their determined faces. He suddenly felt strong again, as if his friends were giving him new energy. He nodded. "You're right. We don't need Commandant Eckles." He draped his arms around Danny and Ruby's shoulders. "And, expelled or not, we have a job to do!"

READ ON FOR A SNEAK
PEEK AT BOOK 12:

REVENGE OF THE
DRAGON

CHAPTER 1

EXPELLED!

"I THINK I've made myself clear," snapped Eckles. "You are expelled!"

"But we were sent here to help the Legion defeat Raina," said Jack. "She's still out there."

Eckles's face twitched. "We can handle Raina quite effectively without you," she said.

She can't really believe that,
thought Jack. *Without us, many of
the Legion would have died already.*

"If I could say something ..." Danny
began. He looked to be in pain. Jack
guessed his bat-like super-sensitive
ears weren't appreciating the volume
of Eckles' telling off.

"No, you may not," said Eckles. "I'm
sending word to Chancellor Rex at the
Hero Academy that you'll be returning
at once."

She turned her back on them, and
marched away, armour clanking as
she descended a set of stairs.

Ruby turned to Jack, her bright

orange eyes aglow with desperation. "What now?"

"I really don't know," he replied quietly.

He thought of Chancellor Rex and how disappointed he'd be. The headmaster wanted Team Hero and the Legion to be allies, but after this incident, that seemed unlikely. *We've really messed things up this time.*

Check out the next book:
REVENGE OF THE DRAGON
to find out what happens next!

IN EVERY BOOK OF
TEAM HERO SERIES
ONE there is a special
Power Token. Collect
all four tokens to get
an exclusive Team Hero
Club pack. The pack
contains everything you and
your friends need to form your
very own Team Hero Club.

MEMBERSHIP CARDS • MEMBERSHIP CERTIFICATE • STICKERS • POWER GAME • BOOKMARKS

Just fill in the form below, send it in with your four tokens
and we'll send you your Team Hero Club Pack.

SEND TO: Team Hero Club Pack Offer, Hachette Children's Books,
Marketing Department, Carmelite House, 50 Victoria Embankment,
London, EC4Y 0DZ.

CLOSING DATE: 31st December 2018

WWW.TEAMHEROBOOKS.CO.UK

Please complete using capital letters *(UK and Republic of Ireland residents only)*

FIRST NAME
SURNAME
DATE OF BIRTH
ADDRESS LINE 1
ADDRESS LINE 2
ADDRESS LINE 3
POSTCODE
PARENT OR GUARDIAN'S EMAIL

I'd like to receive Team Hero email newsletters and information about
other great Hachette Children's Group offers (I can unsubscribe at any time)

*Terms and conditions apply. For full terms and conditions please go to
teamherobooks.co.uk/terms*

*TEAM HERO Club packs
available while stocks last.
Terms and conditions apply.*

COLLECT ALL OF SERIES THREE!

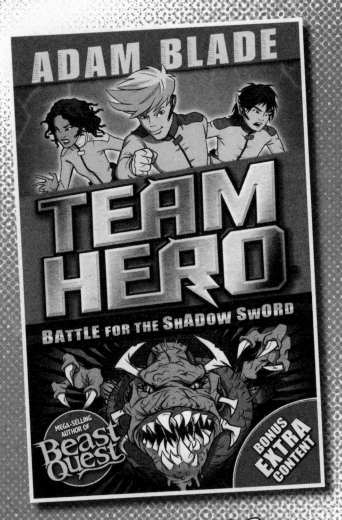

TEAM HERO
BOOK 1
OUT NOW!